W9-BDK-708

Juan Verdades

The Man Who Couldn't Tell a Lie

Juan Verdades

The Man Who Couldn't Tell a Lie

retold by **Joe Hayes**

illustrated by **Joseph Daniel Fiedler**

SCHOLASTIC INC.
New York Toronto London Auckland Sydney
Mexico City New Delhi Hong Kong Buenos Aires

The text of this book is set in 15 point Golden Type bold.
The illustrations are Windsor & Newton alkyd on paper.

No part of this publication may be reproduced in whole or in part, or stored in a retrieval system, or transmitted in any form or by any means,
electronic, mechanical, photocopying, recording, or otherwise, without written permission of the publisher. For information regarding permission,
write to Scholastic Inc., 557 Broadway, New York, NY 10012.

Text copyright © 2001 by Joe Hayes.
Illustrations copyright © 2001 by Joseph Daniel Fiedler.
All rights reserved. Published by Scholastic Inc.
Printed in the U.S.A.

ISBN-13: 978-0-439-92157-2
ISBN-10: 0-439-92157-0

SCHOLASTIC and associated logos and designs are
trademarks and/or registered trademarks of Scholastic Inc.

7 8 9 10 11 12   08   16 17 18 19 20

For all who recognize the truth in the old tales,
whether the story ever happened or not

—J.H.

To Kristy

—J.D.F.

ONE LATE SUMMER DAY a group of wealthy rancheros was gathered on the village plaza, joking and laughing and discussing events on their ranches.

One of the men, whose name was don Ignacio, had a fine apple tree on his land. The rancher called the apple tree *el manzano real*—the royal apple tree—and was extremely proud of it. It had been planted by his great-grandfather, and there was something about the soil it grew in and the way the afternoon sun struck it that made the apple tree flourish. It gave sweeter and more flavorful fruit than any other tree in the country round about.

Every rancher for miles around knew about *el manzano real*, and each year they all hoped don Ignacio would give them a small basket of its sweet fruit. And so each of the ranchers asked don Ignacio how the fruit of the apple tree was doing. To each one don Ignacio replied, "It's doing beautifully, amigo, beautifully. My foreman takes perfect care of the tree, and every evening he reports how the fruit is ripening."

When don Ignacio said this to his friend don Arturo, the other man replied, "Do you mean to say, don Ignacio, that you don't tend your magnificent tree yourself? How can you have such faith in your employee? Maybe he's not doing all he says he is. Maybe he's not telling you the truth."

Don Ignacio wagged a finger at his friend. "*Mi capataz* has never failed me in any way," he insisted. "He has never told me a lie."

"Are you sure, *compadre*?" said don Arturo. "Are you sure that he has never lied to you?"

"Absolutely certain, *compadre*, absolutely certain. The young man doesn't know how to tell a lie. His name is Juan Valdez, but everyone calls him Juan Verdades because he is so truthful."

"I don't believe it. There never was an employee who didn't lie to his boss. I'm sure I can make him tell you a lie."

"Never," replied the proud employer.

The two friends went on arguing good-naturedly, but little by little they began to raise their voices and attract the attention of the other men on the plaza.

Finally don Arturo declared loudly, "I'll bet you whatever you want that within two weeks at the most I'll make this Juan Verdades tell you a lie."

"All right," replied don Ignacio. "It's a deal. I'll bet my ranch against yours that you can't make my foreman lie to me."

The other ranchers laughed when they heard that. "Ho-ho, don Arturo," they said, "now we'll see just how sure you are that you're right."

"As sure as I am of my own name," said don Arturo. "I accept the bet, don Ignacio. But you must allow me the freedom to try anything I wish." The two friends shook hands, and the other men in the group agreed to serve as witnesses to the bet.

The gathering broke up, and don Arturo and don Ignacio rode confidently away toward their ranches. But as don Arturo rode along thinking of what he had just done, he no longer felt so sure of himself. When he arrived home and told his wife and daughter about the bet, his wife began to cry. "What will we do when we lose our ranch?" she sobbed. And don Arturo began to think he had made a terrible mistake.

But his daughter, whose name was Araceli and who was a very bright and lively young woman, just laughed and said, "Don't worry, *Mamá.* We're not going to lose our ranch."

Araceli suggested to her father that he make up some excuse for them all to spend the next two weeks at don Ignacio's house. "If we're staying on don Ignacio's ranch," she said, "we'll surely discover a way to come out the winners."

The next day don Arturo rode to don Ignacio's ranch and told his friend, "My men are mending the walls of my house and giving them a fresh coat of whitewash. It would be more convenient for my family to be away. Could my wife and daughter and I stay at your house for a while?"

"Of course, my friend," don Ignacio answered. "Feel perfectly free."

That afternoon don Arturo and his family moved into don Ignacio's house, and the next morning Araceli rose at dawn, as she always did at home, and went to the ranch kitchen to prepare coffee. The foreman, Juan Verdades, was already there, drinking a cup of coffee he had made for himself and eating a breakfast of leftover tortillas. She smiled at him, and he greeted her politely: *"Buenos días, señorita."* And then he finished his simple breakfast and went off to begin his day's work.

That night don Arturo and his daughter made up a plan. Araceli rose before dawn the next day and went to the kitchen to prepare coffee and fresh tortillas for the foreman. She smiled sweetly as she offered them to Juan. He returned her smile and thanked her very kindly. Each morning she did the same thing, and Juan Verdades began to fall in love with Araceli, which was just what the girl and her father expected.

What Araceli hadn't expected was that she began to fall in love with Juan Verdades too and looked forward to getting up early every morning just to be alone with him. She even began to wish she might end up marrying the handsome young foreman. Araceli continued to work on the plan she and her father had made—but she now had a plan of her own as well.

Of course, Juan knew that he was just a worker and Araceli was the daughter of a wealthy ranchero, so he didn't even dream of asking her to marry him. Still, he couldn't help trying to please her in every way. So one morning when they were talking, Juan said to Araceli, "You're very kind to have fresh coffee and warm food ready for me every morning and to honor me with the pleasure of your company. Ask me for whatever you want from this ranch. I'll speak to don Ignacio and see that it's given to you."

This is exactly what the girl and her father thought would happen. And she replied just as they had planned. It was the last thing Juan expected to hear.

"There's only one thing on this ranch I want," she said. "I'd like to have all the apples from *el manzano real.*"

The young man was very surprised, and very distressed as well, because he knew he couldn't fulfill her wish.

"I could never give you that," Juan said. "You know how don Ignacio treasures the fruit of that tree. He might agree to give you a basket of apples, but no more. I would have to take the fruit without permission, and then what would I say to don Ignacio? I can give you anything else from the ranch, but not what you're asking for."

With that the conversation ended and they separated for the day. In the evening Juan reported to don Ignacio, and they exchanged the exact words they said every evening:

"Good evening, *mi capataz*," the rancher said.

"Good evening, *mi patrón*," replied the foreman.

"How goes it with my cattle and land?"

"Your cattle are healthy, your pastures are green."

"And the fruit of *el manzano real*?"

"The fruit is fat and ripening well."

The next morning Juan and Araceli met again. As they sipped their coffee together, Juan said, "I truly would like to repay you for the kindness you've shown me. There must be something on this ranch you would like. Tell me what it is. I'll see that it's given to you."

But again Araceli replied, "There's only one thing on this ranch I want: the apples from *el manzano real.*"

Each day they repeated the conversation. Araceli asked for the same thing, and Juan said he couldn't give it to her. But each day Juan was falling more hopelessly in love with Araceli. Finally, just the day before the two weeks of the bet would have ended, the foreman gave in. He said he would go pick the apples right then and bring them to the girl.

Juan hitched up a wagon and drove to the apple tree. He picked every single apple and delivered the wagonload of fruit to Araceli. She thanked him very warmly, and his spirits rose for a moment. But as he mounted his horse to leave, they sank once again. Juan rode away alone, lost in his thoughts, and Araceli hurried off to tell her father the news and then to wait for a chance to talk to don Ignacio too.

Juan rode until he came to a place where there were several dead trees. He dismounted and walked up to one of them. Then he took off his hat and jacket and put them on the dead tree and pretended it was don Ignacio. He started talking to it to see if he could tell it a lie.

"Good evening, *mi capataz*," he pretended he heard the tree say.

"Good evening, *mi patrón*."

"How goes it with my cattle and land?"

"Your cattle are healthy, your pastures are green."

"And the fruit of *el manzano real*?"

"The . . . the crows have carried the fruit away. . . ."

But the words were hardly out of his mouth when he heard himself say, "No, that's not true, *mi patrón*. I picked the fruit. . . ." And then he stopped himself.

He took a deep breath and started over again with, "Good evening, *mi capataz*."

And when he reached the end, he sputtered, "The . . . the wind shook the apples to the ground, and the cows came and ate them. . . . No, they didn't, *mi patrón*. I . . ."

He tried over and over, until he realized there was no way he could tell a lie. But he knew he could never come right out and say what he had done either. He had to think of another way to tell don Ignacio. He took his hat and coat from the stump and sadly set out for the ranch.

All day long Juan worried about what he would say to don Ignacio. And all day long don Ignacio wondered what he would hear from his foreman, because as soon as Araceli had shown the apples to her father he had run gleefully to tell don Ignacio what had happened.

"Now you'll see, *compadre*," don Arturo gloated. "You're about to hear a lie from Juan Verdades."

Don Ignacio was heartsick to think that all his apples had been picked, but he had agreed that don Arturo could try whatever he wanted. He sighed and said, "Very well, *compadre*, we'll see what happens this evening."

Don Arturo rode off to gather the other ranchers who were witnesses to the bet, leaving don Ignacio to pace nervously up and down in his house. And then, after don Ignacio received a visit from Araceli and she made a request that he couldn't deny, he paced even more nervously.

All the while, Juan went about his work, thinking of what he would say to his don Ignacio. That evening the foreman went as usual to make his report to his employer, but he walked slowly and his head hung down. The other ranchers were behind the bushes listening, and Araceli and her mother were watching anxiously from a window of the house.

The conversation began as it always did:

"Good evening, *mi capataz*."

"Good evening, *mi patrón*."

"How goes it with my cattle and land?"

"Your cattle are healthy, your pastures are green."

"And the fruit of *el manzano real*?"

Juan took a deep breath and replied:

"Oh, *patrón*, something terrible happened today.

Some fool picked your apples and gave them away."

Don Ignacio pretended to be shocked and confused. "Some fool picked them?" he said. "Who would do such a thing?"

Juan turned his face aside. He couldn't look at don Ignacio. The rancher asked again, "Who would do such a thing? Do I know this person?"

Finally the foreman answered:

"The father of the fool is my father's father's son.

The fool has no sister and no brother.

His child would call my father 'grandfather.'

He's ashamed that he did what was done."

Don Ignacio paused for a moment to think about Juan's answer. And then, to Juan's surprise, don Ignacio grabbed his hand and started shaking it excitedly.

The other ranchers ran laughing from their hiding places. "Don Arturo," they all said, "you lose the bet. You must sign your ranch over to don Ignacio."

"No," said don Ignacio, still vigorously shaking Juan's hand. He glanced toward the window where Araceli was watching and went on: "Sign it over to don Juan Verdades. He has proved that he truly deserves that name, and he deserves to be the owner of his own ranch as well."

Everyone cheered and began to congratulate Juan. Don Arturo's face turned white, but he gritted his teeth and forced a smile. He shook Juan's hand and then turned to walk away from the group, his shoulders drooping and his head bowed down.

But Araceli came running from the house and put her arm through her father's. "*Papá,*" she said, "what if Juan Verdades were to marry a relative of yours? Then the ranch would stay in the family, wouldn't it?"

Everyone heard her and turned to look at the girl and her father. And then Juan spoke up confidently. "*Señorita* Araceli, I am the owner of a ranch and many cattle. Will you marry me?"

Of course she said she would, and don Arturo heaved a great sigh. "Don Juan Verdades," he said, "I'll be proud to have such an honest man for a son-in-law." He beckoned his wife to come from the house, and they both hugged Juan and Araceli.

The other ranchers hurried off to fetch their families, and a big celebration began. It lasted all through the night, with music and dancing and many toasts to Juan and Araceli. And in the morning everyone went home with a big basket of delicious apples from *el manzano real.*

Note to Readers and Storytellers

The origin of the tale I call "Juan Verdades" is clearly European. The story turns up in many lands and languages. It is a variant of tale number 889 ("The Faithful Servant") in the Aarne-Thompson index of tale types. Early in the twentieth century, a version was collected in Spain by Aurelio M. Espinosa and published in *Cuentos populares españoles*. In the 1920s two versions were found in New Mexico by Juan B. Rael and included in his monumental work *Cuentos españoles de Colorado y Nuevo México*. The tale has been collected in Latin America as well.

In telling "Juan Verdades," I have given the tale a more literary treatment than I usually do. For example, I have assigned names to all of the principal characters so that the reader can keep them straight. In a traditional telling, only the main character would be given a name, and even he might simply be identified as *el joven* or *el muchacho*. I have also used dialogue to carry the narrative and clarify the characters' motivations to a greater extent than would be found in a true folktale.

Finally, I have changed the content of the story a bit. In traditional versions the daughter isn't a strong character. She just follows her father's orders. The prized possession of the employer is usually an animal, a bull or an ox, and the girl demands that it be killed and served to her. In my retelling I have softened her request. The final riddle spoken by Juan is my invention, but the conversation in verse between the servant and master is traditional. And the episode of the young man talking to a tree or a stump seems especially typical of Hispanic versions of the tale. It was the element that first captured my imagination and made me want to retell the story.